melville house classics

THE ART OF THE NOVELLA

A SIMPLE HEART

A SIMPLE HEART

GUSTAVE FLAUBERT

TRANSLATED BY CHARLOTTE MANDELL

MELVILLE HOUSE PUBLISHING
HOBOKEN, NEW JERSEY

"A SIMPLE HEART" WAS FIRST PUBLISHED IN FRENCH AS "UN COEUR SIMPLE" IN *TROIS CONTES (THREE TALES)* IN 1877.

BOOK DESIGN: DAVID KONOPKA

MELVILLE HOUSE PUBLISHING
46 JOHN STREET
BROOKLYN, NY 11201
WWW.MHPBOOKS.COM

THIRD MELVILLE HOUSE PRINTING: MAY 2015
ISBN: 978-0-974607-88-7

LIBRARY OF CONGRESS CATALOGING-IN-PUBLICATION DATA ON FILE.

A SIMPLE HEART

I

For half a century, the housewives of Pont-l'Évêque envied Madame Aubain her servant, Félicité.

For a hundred francs a year, she did the cooking and cleaning, sewed, did the laundry, ironed, knew how to bridle a horse, fatten fowl, churn butter, and remained loyal to her mistress—who, however, was not a pleasant person.

Madame Aubain had married a handsome bachelor without a fortune, who died at the beginning of 1809, leaving her with two very young children and a number of debts. So she sold her properties, except the Toucques farm and the Geffosses farm, the income from which amounted to 5,000 francs at most, and she left her Saint-Melaine house to go live in another more economical one, which had belonged to her forebears and was located behind the market-place.

This house, roofed with slate, was between an alleyway and a little lane ending at the river. Inside, it had varying levels, which made for stumbling. A narrow hallway separated the kitchen from the "parlor" where Madame Aubain stayed all throughout the day, seated next to the casement window in a wicker armchair. Against the wainscoting, painted white, eight mahogany chairs were lined up. An old piano supported, beneath a barometer, a pyramidal stack of boxes and cartons. Two tapestried wing-chairs flanked the yellow marble, Louix XV mantelpiece. The clock at the center represented a Temple of Vesta—and the whole room smelled a little of mold, since the floor was lower than the garden.

On the second floor, there was first "Madame's" bedroom, very large, hung with a wallpaper of pale flowers, and containing the portrait of "Monsieur," dressed in a foppish outfit. It communicated with a smaller bedroom, where two children's cots were to be seen, without mattresses. Then came the sitting-room, always closed, and filled with furniture covered with a sheet. Then a hallway led to a study; books and papers ranged the shelves of a bookcase that surrounded the three sides of a large desk in black wood. The two end panels disappeared beneath ink drawings, landscapes in gouache, and engravings by Audran, remembrances from a better time and a vanished luxury. A dormer window on the third floor gave light to Félicité's room, which looked out onto the meadows.

She rose at dawn, in order not to miss Mass, and worked until evening without interruption; then, dinner over, the dishes put away and the door firmly closed, she would bury the log under the ashes and fall asleep in front of the hearth, her rosary in her hand. No one, in bargaining, showed more stubbornness. When it came to cleanliness, the gleam of her pots made other servants despair. Thrifty, she ate slowly, and with her finger on the table gathered together the crumbs from her bread—a loaf that weighed twelve pounds, baked specially for her, which lasted for twenty days.

All year round she wore a printed calico kerchief fastened in back with a pin, a bonnet that hid her hair, grey stockings, a red skirt, and over her blouse an apron with a bib, like a hospital nurse.

Her face was thin and her voice shrill. At the age of twenty-five, she looked forty. After she turned fifty, she no longer showed any age;—and, always silent, her posture straight and her gestures measured, she seemed like a woman made of wood, functioning in an automatic way.

II

She had had, like any other woman, her love affair. Her father, a stonemason, had been killed when he fell from a scaffold. Then her mother died; her sisters scattered; a farmer took her in, and hired her, still a little girl, to watch over the cows in the fields. She shivered under rags, drank pondwater stretched out on her stomach, was beaten for the least thing, and finally was chased away for a theft of thirty *sous*, which she hadn't committed. She entered service at another farm, there took care of the poultry, and, since the owners liked her, her fellow workers were jealous of her.

One evening in August (she was then eighteen years old), they took her to the fair at Colleville.

Right away she was dazed, stupefied by the racket of the fiddlers, the lights in the trees, the loud colors of the outfits, the lace, the golden crosses, this crush of people leaping about all at once. She was modestly keeping herself out of the way, when a young man who looked well-off, and who was smoking his pipe, both his elbows on the shaft of a cart, came to invite her to dance. He bought her cider, coffee, cake, a kerchief, and, thinking she guessed his intentions, offered to take her home. On the edge of a field of oats, he threw her down suddenly. She was afraid and began to scream. He took himself off.

Another evening, on the Beaumont road, she wanted to pass a big hay wagon that was going slowly, and as she brushed against the wheels she recognized Théodore.

He approached her calmly, saying she should forgive everything, since it was "the fault of the drink."

She didn't know what to reply and wanted to run away.

Immediately he spoke of the harvest and the noteworthy people of the community, for his father had left Colleville for the Écots farm, so that now they were neighbors. "Ah!" she said. He added they wanted him to settle down. But he was in no hurry, and would wait for a woman to his liking. She lowered her head. Then he asked her if she thought about marriage. She replied, smiling, that it was mean to make fun of her.

"But no, I swear it!" and with his left arm he encircled her waist; she walked supported by his embrace; they slowed down. The wind was gentle, the stars were shining, the enormous cartload of hay swayed in front of them; and the four horses, dragging their steps, stirred up dust. Then, without an order, they turned right. He kissed her one more time. She disappeared into the shadow.

Théodore, the following week, won several meetings with her.

They would meet at the back of farmyards, or behind a wall, or under a remote tree. She was not innocent in the way young ladies are—animals had instructed her;—but reason and the instinct of honor prevented her from succumbing. This resistance exasperated Théodore's love so much that to satisfy it (or perhaps ingenuously) he offered to marry her. She was hesitant to believe him. He made solemn promises.

Soon he confessed an unfortunate thing: his parents, last year, had hired a substitute to do his military service; but from one day to the next this privilege could be taken away from him; the idea of serving terrified him. This cowardice was for Félicité a proof of tenderness; her own was redoubled. She would slip out at night, and, when she reached the meeting-place, Théodore would torment her with his anxieties and his entreaties.

Finally, he announced that he would go to the Prefecture himself to get information, and would return with it next Sunday, between eleven and midnight.

When the time came, she ran to her sweetheart.

In his place, she found one of his friends.

He told her that she would see him no more. To save himself from conscription, Théodore had married a very rich old woman, Madame Lehoussais, from Toucques.

Her grief was uncontrollable. She threw herself on the ground, screamed, called on the good Lord, and groaned all alone in the field until sunrise. Then she returned to the farm and declared her intention to leave it; and, at the end of the month, having received her wages, she tied up all her few belongings in a bandana, and went to Pont-l'Évêque.

In front of the inn, she questioned a housewife in a widow's cap, who was in fact looking for a cook. The girl didn't know much, but seemed to have so much good will and so few requirements that Madame Aubain ended up saying, "So be it, I'll take you!"

A quarter of an hour later, Félicité was settled in her house.

At first she lived there in a sort of trembling brought on by "the sort of house" it was, and by the memory of "Monsieur," hovering over everything! Paul and Virginie, one seven years of age, the other scarcely four, seemed to her formed from a precious substance; she carried them on her back like a horse, and Madame Aubain forbade her to kiss them every minute, which mortified her. But she was happy. The gentleness of her surroundings had dissolved her sadness.

Every Thursday, the regulars would come to play a game of boston. Félicité prepared the cards and foot-warmers in advance. They arrived at eight o'clock precisely, and left before it struck eleven.

Every Monday morning, the secondhand goods dealer who lived down the lane spread out his scrap iron on the ground. Then the town was filled with the buzz of voices, in which the neighing of horses, the bleating of lambs, the grunts of pigs mingled with the harsh noise of carts in the street. Around noon, at the height of the market, there would appear on the doorstep an old peasant of tall stature, his cap pushed back, his nose hooked; this was Robelin, the farmer from Geffosses. Soon afterwards, Liébard would appear, the farmer from Toucques, small, red, obese, wearing a grey jacket and chaps furnished with spurs.

Both of them would offer their landlady hens or cheeses. Félicité invariably foiled their tricks; and they would leave full of respect for her.

At irregular intervals, Madame Aubain would receive a visit from the Marquis de Gremanville, one of her uncles, ruined by dissolution, who lived in Falaise on the last parcel of his lands. He would always appear at lunch-time, with a hideous poodle whose paws dirtied all the furniture. Despite his efforts to seem a gentleman, going so far as to raise his hat every time he said "My late father," habit won out, and he would pour himself cup after cup to drink, and let slip ribald remarks. Félicité would politely push him out: "You have had enough, Monsieur de Gremanville! Till another time!" And she would close the door.

She would open it with pleasure to Monsieur Bourais, a former solicitor. His white cravat and his baldness, the jabot of his shirt, his ample brown frock coat, the way he had of curling his arm round as he took snuff, his entire person produced in her that confusion into which the sight of extraordinary men throws us.

Since he looked after "Madame's" properties, he would shut himself up with her for hours in "Monsieur's" study, always feared compromising himself, had an infinite respect for the magistracy, and had pretensions to Latin.

To educate the children in a pleasant way, he made them the gift of a geography book with illustrations. These represented different scenes around the world, cannibals with feather headdresses, a monkey carrying off a maiden, Bedouins in the desert, a whale being harpooned, etc.

Paul gave the explanation of these plates to Félicité. This was in fact her whole literary education.

The children's education was handled by Guyot, a poor devil employed in the town hall, famous for his fine writing hand, who honed his penknife on his boot.

When the weather was clear, they would leave early for the farm of Geffosses.

The farmyard is sloping, the house in the middle; and the sea, in the distance, looks like a grey stain.

Félicité took out of her market basket slices of cold meat, and they lunched in a room connected to the dairy. It was all that remained of a summer house, now vanished. The tattered paper on the wall trembled in the drafts. Madame Aubain bent down her forehead, overwhelmed with memories; the children didn't dare speak. "Go out and play!" she said; they ran off.

Paul climbed into the barn, trapped birds, skipped pebbles on the pond, or banged with a stick the big barrels that resounded like drums.

Virginie fed the rabbits, hurried off to gather

blueberries, and the quickness of her legs revealed her little embroidered knickers.

One evening in autumn, they came home through the pastures.

The moon in its first quarter lit up a part of the sky, and a mist floated like a shawl over the meanderings of the river Toucques. Oxen, stretched out in the middle of the field, calmly watched these four people go by. In the third pasture a few of them got up, then ranged themselves in a circle in front of them. "Do not be afraid!" said Félicité; and, murmuring a sort of lament, she stroked the back of the one closest to her; he did an about-face, and the others imitated him. But, when the next pasture had been crossed, a tremendous lowing arose. It was a bull, which had been hidden by the fog. He came towards the two women. Madame Aubain was going to run. "No! No! Don't move so fast!" But they hurried their steps, and heard behind them a loud breathing coming nearer. His hooves, like hammers, beat the grass in the field; now he was galloping! Félicité turned around, and with both hands she tore up clods of earth that she threw in his eyes. He lowered his muzzle, shook his horns and trembled with fury, bellowing horribly. Madame Aubain, at the edge of the pasture with her little ones, sought frantically to climb over the high bank. Félicité steadily retreated in front of the bull, and kept throwing lumps of turf that blinded him, while she shouted: "Hurry! Hurry!"

Madame Aubain clambered down the ditch, pushed Virginie, then Paul, fell many times while trying to climb the slope, and by sheer willpower managed it.

The bull had driven Félicité back against a fence; his spittle was spraying her face, one more second and he would disembowel her. She had just enough time to slip between two railings, and the huge animal, completely surprised, stopped.

This event, for many years, was a subject of conversation in Pont-l'Évêque. Félicité drew no pride from it, not even thinking she had done anything heroic.

Virginie occupied her exclusively—for, as a result of her fright, she had a nervous ailment, and M. Poupart, the doctor, advised bathing in the sea at Trouville.

At that time, it was not much frequented. Madame Aubain made inquiries, consulted Bourais, made preparations as if for a long voyage.

Her luggage left the day before, in Liébard's cart. The next day, he brought two horses, one of which had a lady's saddle, fitted out with a velvet back; and on the crupper of the second a rolled-up coat formed a kind of seat. Madame Aubain mounted it, behind him. Félicité took charge of Virginie, and Paul mounted M. Lechaptois' donkey, lent on the condition that they would take great care of it.

The road was so bad that its eight kilometers required two hours. The horses sank down to their pasterns in the mud, and to get out of it made sudden movements with their haunches; or else they stumbled over ruts; other times, they had to jump. Liébard's mare, at certain places, would stop all of a sudden. He would patiently wait for her to start up again; and he would speak of the people whose properties lined the road, adding moral reflections to their histories. Thus, in the middle of Toucques, as they were passing under windows surrounded by nasturtiums, he said, shrugging his shoulders: "There's a woman, Madame Lehoussais, who instead of taking a young man..." Félicité didn't hear the rest; the horses trotted, the donkey galloped; they all filed up a path, a gate swung open, two boys appeared, and they dismounted in front of the dungheap run-off, right at the doorstep.

Old Mother Liébard, seeing her mistress, was lavish with demonstrations of joy. She served her a lunch that included sirloin, tripe, blood sausage, chicken fricassee, frothy cider, a tart of stewed fruit, and plums in brandy, accompanying everything with polite remarks to Madame who seemed in the best of health, to Mademoiselle who had turned out "wonderful," to M. Paul remarkably "strengthened," without forgetting their dead grandparents whom the Liébards had known, having been in the service of the family for many generations. The farm had, like them, an ancient quality. The roof beams were worm-eaten, the walls black with smoke, the floor tiles grey with dust. An oak dresser supported all sorts of utensils, pitchers, plates, pewter bowls, wolf-traps, sheep shears; an enormous syringe made the children laugh. There wasn't a tree in the three courtyards that didn't have mushrooms at its base, or in its branches a cluster of mistletoe. The wind had toppled many of them. They had taken root again from the middle; and they all sagged under the abundance of their apples. The straw roofs, like brown velvet and of varying thicknesses, resisted the strongest gusts. The wagon-shed, however, was falling in ruins. Madame Aubain said she would take note, and ordered the animals to be reharnessed.

Another half-hour went by before they reached Trouville. The little caravan dismounted to pass "Les Écores"; this was a cliff overhanging the boats; and three minutes later, at the end of the quay, they entered the courtyard of "The Golden Lamb," kept by old Mother David.

Virginie, after the first few days, felt less weak, a result of the change of air and the effects of the baths. She took them in her shift, for lack of a bathing costume; and her maid dressed her in a customs shed used by the bathers.

In the afternoon, they went with the donkey beyond the Black Rocks, near Hennequeville. The path, at first, rose between undulating lands like the lawn of a park, then arrived at a plateau where pastures and plowed fields alternated. On the edge of the path, in the tangle of brambles, holly rose up; here and there, a big dead tree crisscrossed the blue air with its boughs.

Almost always they would rest in a meadow, with Deauville on their left, Le Havre on their right, and facing them the open sea. It gleamed in the sun, smooth as a mirror, so gentle one could scarcely hear its murmur; hidden sparrows chirruped and the immense vault of heaven covered it all. Madame Aubain, seated, worked on her sewing; Virginie next to her plaited reeds; Félicité pulled up lavender flowers; Paul, who was bored, wanted to leave.

Other times, having crossed the river Toucques in a boat, they looked for shells. The low tide left exposed sea urchins, sea-ears, jellyfish; and the children ran to grab the flecks of foam the wind was carrying away. The drowsy waves, falling onto the sand, rolled back all along the shore; it stretched out as far as the eye could see, but on the land side had a border of dunes that separated it from the "Marsh," a wide meadow in the shape of a race-track. When they came back that way, Trouville, in the distance on the slope of a hill, grew larger at each step, and with all its disparate houses seemed to spread out in a cheerful disorder.

On days when it was too hot, they did not leave their room. The dazzling brilliance from outside plastered bars of light between the slats of the blinds. Not a sound in the village. Down below, on the sidewalk, no one. This spreading silence increased the tranquility of things. In the distance, the caulkers' hammers tamped the hulls, and a heavy breeze brought the smell of tar.

The chief amusement was the return of the fishing-boats. As soon as they had passed the channel markers, they began to tack. The sails came down the masts two-thirds of the way; and, with their foresails swollen like a balloon, they came forward, sliding through the lapping waves, into the middle of the harbor, where suddenly they dropped anchor. Then the boat took its place against the quay. The sailors threw onto the planks the quivering fish; a line of handcarts awaited them, and women in cotton bonnets rushed forward to take the baskets and embrace their husbands.

One of these women, one day, approached Félicité, who soon afterwards came into the room full of joy. She had found a sister; and Nastasie Barette, Leroux's wife, appeared, with an infant at her breast, in her right hand another child, and at her left a little sailor boy, his fists on his hips and his beret over his ear.

After a quarter of an hour, Madame Aubain dismissed her.

They could always be found hanging about the kitchen, or strolling together outside. The husband never showed himself.

Félicité developed a fondness for them. She bought them a blanket, some shirts, a stove; obviously they were taking advantage of her. This weakness annoyed Madame Aubain, who moreover did not like the familiarities of the nephew—for he addressed her son as "tu";—and, since Virginie was coughing and the season was no longer fair, she returned to Pont-l'Évêque.

M. Bourais enlightened her on the choice of a school. The one in Caen was regarded as the best. Paul was sent there, and bravely said his goodbyes, pleased he was going to live in a house where he would have friends.

Madame Aubain resigned herself to the separation from her son, because it was necessary. Virginie thought about him less and less. Félicité missed his commotion. But an occupation came to distract her; starting at Christmas, she took the little girl every day to catechism class.

III When she had genuflected at the door, she came forward down the high nave, between the two ranks of chairs, opened Madame Aubain's pew, sat down, and let her eyes rove around her.

The boys on the right, the girls on the left, filled the stalls of the choir; the priest remained standing next to the lectern; in a stained-glass window in the apse, the Holy Ghost looked down on the Virgin; another showed her kneeling in front of the Infant Jesus, and, behind the tabernacle, a group carved in wood represented Saint Michael bringing down the dragon.

The priest first summarized sacred History. She thought she could see paradise, the flood, the

Tower of Babel, the cities all in flames, the peoples who were dying, the idols knocked down; and from this bedazzlement she retained a respect for the Most High and fear of his wrath. Then she cried while hearing about the Passion. Why had they crucified him, he who cherished children, fed the multitudes, cured the blind, and had chosen, out of gentleness, to be born in the midst of the poor, on the dunghill of a stable? Sowings, harvests, wine presses, all those familiar things the Gospel speaks of, existed in her life; the passage of God had sanctified them; and she loved lambs more tenderly for love of the Lamb, doves because of the Holy Ghost.

She found it difficult to imagine his appearance; for he was not only a bird, but also a fire, and other times a breath. It might be his light that flutters about at night on the edges of swamps, his breathing that pushes the clouds, his voice that makes bells harmonious; and she remained in adoration, taking pleasure in the coolness of the walls and the tranquility of the church.

As to the dogmas, she understood none of them, didn't even try to understand. The priest discoursed, the children recited, she ended up falling asleep; and awoke all of a sudden, when their clogs rang out on the flagstones as they were leaving.

It was in this way, by dint of listening to it, that she learned the catechism, her religious education having been neglected in her youth; and from then on she imitated all the practices of Virginie, fasted as she did, went to confession with her. At Corpus Christi, they made an altar together.

The first communion worried her beforehand. She bustled about for the shoes, for the rosary, for the book, for the gloves. With what trembling did she help the mother dress her!

Throughout the whole Mass, she was full of anxiety. M. Bourais hid part of the choir from her; but just opposite, the flock of virgins wearing white wreaths over their lowered veils formed what looked like a field of snow; and she recognized from afar the dear little one from her dainty neck and her contemplative bearing. The bell tinkled. Heads were bent; there was a silence. To the booming of the organ, the soloists and the crowd intoned the Agnus Dei; then the procession of boys began; and, after them, the girls stood. Step by step, their palms joined, they went towards the brightly lit altar, knelt down on the first step, one after the other received the Host, and then in the same order returned to their kneelers. When it was Virginie's turn, Félicité bent forward to see her; and, with the imagination that comes with real tenderness, it seemed to her that she herself was this child; her face became her own, her dress clothed her, her heart beat in her chest; when the time came to open her mouth, as she closed her eyes, she almost fainted.

The next day, quite early, she presented herself in the sacristy, so that the priest could give her communion. She received it devoutly, but did not taste the same delight in it.

Madame Aubain wanted to make an accomplished person of her daughter; and, as Guyot could give her neither English nor music, she resolved to send her to boarding school with the Ursulines of Honfleur.

The child had no objections. Félicité sighed, thinking Madame insensitive. Then she thought her mistress might be right. These things were beyond her understanding.

Finally, one day, an old wagon stopped in front of the door; and a nun stepped out of it who had come to fetch Mademoiselle. Félicité loaded the luggage onto the roof of the carriage, gave advice to the coachman, and stowed under the seat six pots of jam and a dozen pears, along with a bouquet of violets.

Virginie, at the last minute, was taken with a fit of sobbing; she embraced her mother, who kissed her on the forehead, repeating, "Come now! Be brave! Be brave!" The running board was raised, and the coach left.

Then Madame Aubain had a fainting spell; and in the evening all her friends, the Lormeau household, Madame Lechaptois, the Rochefeuille ladies, Monsieur de Houppeville, and Bourais paid a call to console her.

The absence of her daughter was at first very painful for her. But three times each week she received a letter from her; on the other days she wrote to her, took walks in her garden, read a little, and in this way filled the void of the hours.

In the morning, out of habit, Félicité would enter Virginie's bedroom and look at the walls. She missed combing her hair, lacing her boots, tucking her into bed—and no longer constantly seeing her sweet face, no longer holding her hand when they went out together. In her lack of anything to do, she tried to make lace. Her clumsy fingers broke the threads; she couldn't make sense of anything, lost sleep, and, in her words, was "eaten away."

To "clear herself up," she asked permission to receive her nephew Victor.

He would arrive on Sunday after Mass, his cheeks pink, his chest bare, smelling of the countryside he had crossed. Right away, she would set the table. They would lunch facing each other; and, eating as little as possible herself to spare the expense, she stuffed him with so much food that he would end up falling asleep. At the first bell for vespers, she would wake him up, brush his trousers, tie his cravat, and go to church, leaning on his arm with maternal pride.

His parents always told him to get something from her, whether it be a package of brown sugar, or soap, or brandy, sometimes even money. He brought her his worn clothes to mend; and she accepted this chore, glad of an occasion to make him come back.

In August, his father took him away in a coastal schooner.

It was vacation time. The arrival of the children consoled her. But Paul was becoming temperamental, and Virginie was too old to be addressed as "tu," which set an embarrassment, a barrier between them.

Victor went successively to Morlaix, to Dunkirk, and to Brighton; upon returning from each voyage, he would present her with a gift. The first time, it was a box made of shells; the second, a coffee-cup; the third, a big gingerbread man. He was growing more handsome, with a neat waist, a little moustache, nice candid eyes, and a little leather cap, set back on his head like a skipper's. He amused her by telling her stories sprinkled with nautical terms.

One Monday, on July 14, 1819 (she never forgot the date), Victor announced that he had signed on for a long cruise, and, two days from then at night, by the Honfleur boat, he would join his schooner, which was due to cast off from Le Havre shortly. He could be gone for two years, possibly.

The prospect of such an absence devastated Félicité; and to say goodbye to him again, on Wednesday evening, after Madame's dinner, she put on her clogs and ate up the nine miles that separated Pont-l'Évêque from Honfleur.

When she reached the wayside shrine, instead of going left, she went right, got lost in the shipyards, retraced her steps; the people she accosted urged her to hurry. She went all around the docks filled with ships, bumped into the hawsers; then the land sloped down, lights intertwined, and she thought she was going crazy, seeing horses in the sky.

On the edge of the quay, other horses neighed, frightened by the sea. A hoist that was lifting them put them down in a boat, where passengers jostled each other between casks of cider, baskets of cheese, sacks of grain; you could hear chickens clucking, the captain swearing; and a cabin-boy stood leaning on the cathead, indifferent to it all. Félicité, who had not recognized him, shouted, "Victor!" He raised his head; she rushed forward, when all of a sudden they raised the gangway.

The boat, towed by women who were singing, left the port. Its frame creaked, the heavy waves whipped its prow. The sail had come about, you couldn't see anyone anymore;—and, on the sea silvered by the moon, it became a black spot that kept getting paler, gave way, disappeared.

Félicité, passing by the wayside shrine, wanted to commend to God what she cherished most; and she prayed for a long time, standing, her face bathed in tears, her eyes turned up to the clouds. The town slept, customs inspectors strolled; and water fell without stopping through the holes in the lock, with the sound of a torrent. Two o'clock struck.

The visiting-room wouldn't open before daylight. Delay would, of course, annoy Madame; so, despite her wish to embrace the other child, she headed home. The girls at the inn were waking up as she entered Pont-l'Évêque.

The poor boy was going to be tossed on the waves for months, then! His previous voyages hadn't frightened her. From England and Brittany, people came back; but America, the Colonies, the West Indies—they were lost in an uncertain region, on the other side of the world.

From then on, Félicité thought solely of her nephew. On sunny days, she worried about thirst; when there was a thunderstorm, feared lightning for him. Listening to the wind moaning in the chimney and carrying off roof tiles, she saw him battered by this same storm, on top of a shattered mast, his whole body bent backwards, under a sheet of foam; or else—remembering the illustrated geography book—he was being eaten by savages, caught in a forest by monkeys, was dying on a deserted beach. And she never spoke of her anxieties.

Madame Aubain had others about her daughter.

The good sisters thought she was affectionate, but delicate. The least emotion enervated her. She had to give up the piano.

Her mother demanded of the convent a regular correspondence. One morning when the mailman had not come, she became impatient; and she walked around the room, from her armchair to the window. It was really extraordinary! For four days, no news!

To console her by her example, Félicité said to her:

"As for me, Madame, it's been six months now that I haven't gotten any news!"

"From whom?"

The servant gently replied:

"Why... from my nephew!"

"Oh! Your nephew!"

And, shrugging her shoulders, Madame Aubain resumed her pacing, which meant: "I wasn't thinking about him! What's more, I couldn't care less about him! A cabin-boy, a pauper, that's not important. Whereas my daughter.... Think about it!"

Félicité, although brought up on rudeness, was indignant at Madame, and then forgot about it.

It seemed to her quite normal to lose one's head about the little girl.

The two children had an equal importance; a bond from her heart linked them together, and their fate ought to be the same.

The pharmacist told her that Victor's boat had arrived in Havana. He had read this information in a newspaper.

Because of the cigars, she imagined Havana to be a country where one did nothing else but smoke, and Victor was walking about among black people in a cloud of tobacco. Could one "in an emergency" return from there by land? How far was it from Pont-l'Évêque? To find out, she questioned M. Bourais.

He got out his atlas, then began explanations about longitude; and he had a fine pedantic smile at Félicité's stupefaction. Finally, with his pencil-holder, he indicated an imperceptible black dot in the jagged outlines of an oval patch, adding, "Here it is." She leaned over the map; this network of colored lines tired her eyesight without teaching her anything; and, when Bourais asked her to say what was bothering her, she begged him to show her the house where Victor was living. Bourais raised his arms, sneezed, laughed uproariously; such naivety aroused his joy; and Félicité didn't understand the reason for it, she who was perhaps expecting to see all the way down to the image of her nephew, so limited was her intelligence!

It was two weeks later that Liébard, as usual during market-time, came into the kitchen, and gave her a letter sent by her brother-in-law. Since neither of them knew how to read, she appealed to her mistress.

Madame Aubain, who was counting the stitches in her knitting, put it down next to her, opened the letter, shivered, and, in a low voice, with a solemn look:

"It is a misfortune... that they are telling you about. Your nephew..."

He was dead. It didn't say anything else.

Félicité fell onto a chair, leaning her head on the wall, and closed her eyelids, which immediately turned pink. Then, her brow lowered, her hands dangling, her gaze fixed, she repeated at intervals:

"Poor little boy! Poor little boy!"

Liébard observed her and sighed. Madame Aubain trembled a little.

She suggested she go see her sister, in Trouville.

Félicité replied, with a gesture, that there was no need for that.

There was a silence. The good Liébard thought it suitable to withdraw.

Then she said:

"It doesn't affect them at all!"

Her head dropped again; and mechanically she would pick up, from time to time, the long needles on the work table.

Some women passed by in the courtyard carrying a drying frame from which laundry dripped.

Seeing them through the window, she remembered her washing; having set it to soak the day before, she had to rinse it today; and she left the room.

Her washboard and tub were at the shore of the river Touques. She threw on the bank a pile of shirts, rolled up her sleeves, picked up her beater; and the strong blows she gave could be heard in the other gardens nearby. The meadows were empty, the wind troubled the river; in the distance, tall grasses leaned over it, like the hair of corpses floating in the water. She held in her sorrow, and until nightfall was very brave; but, in her bedroom, she abandoned herself to it, on her stomach on the mattress, her face in the pillow, both fists against her temples.

Much later, from Victor's captain himself, she learned the circumstances of his end. They had bled him too much at the hospital, for yellow fever. Four doctors were handling him at once. He had died immediately, and the head doctor had said, "There goes another one!"

His parents had always treated him coarsely. She preferred not to see them again; and they did not make any advances, out of forgetfulness, or from the callousness of the poor.

Virginie was weakening.

Feelings of suffocation, coughing, steady fever and mottling in her cheeks indicated some deep-seated ailment. M. Poupart had advised a stay in Provence. Madame Aubain decided on this, and would have immediately taken her daughter back home, if it were not for the climate of Pont-l'Évêque.

She made an arrangement with a renter of carriages, who took her to the convent every Tuesday. In the garden there is a terrace from which you can glimpse the Seine. Virginie would stroll there on her arm, on the fallen vine leaves. Sometimes the sun crossing the clouds forced her to squint her eyes, while she watched the sails in the distance and the whole horizon, from the chateau of Tancarville to the lighthouses of Le Havre. Then they would rest under the arbor. Her mother had brought a little cask of excellent Malaga wine; and, laughing at the idea of being tipsy, she drank two fingers of it, no more.

Her strength reappeared. Fall passed gently. Félicité reassured Madame Aubain. But, one evening when she had gone shopping in the neighborhood, in front of the door she found the gig of M. Poupart; and he was in the hall. Madame Aubain was tying on her hat.

"Give me my foot-warmer, my purse, my gloves; move quickly now!"

Virginie had an inflammation of the chest; it might be hopeless.

"Not yet!" said the doctor; and they both climbed into the carriage, beneath the swirling snowflakes. Night was falling. It was very cold.

Félicité hurried into the church, to light a candle. Then she ran after the gig, which she reached an hour later, and sprang nimbly onto the back, where she held onto the straps, when a thought came to her: "The courtyard wasn't locked! What if thieves got into it?" And she got down.

The next day, at dawn, she appeared at the doctor's. He had returned, and left again for the country. So she stayed in the inn, thinking some strangers might bring a letter. Finally, at daybreak, she took the coach to Lisieux.

The convent was at the bottom of a steep lane. In the middle of the lane, she heard strange sounds, a death knell. "It's for somebody else," she thought; and Félicité violently plied the knocker.

After several minutes, there was a shuffling of slippers, the door opened halfway, and a nun appeared.

The good sister said with an air of compunction that "she had just passed." At the same time, the knell of Saint-Léonard was redoubled.

Félicité reached the second floor.

From the door to the bedroom, she saw Virginie stretched out on her back, her hands clasped, her mouth open, and her head leaning back under a black cross tilted down towards her, between motionless curtains not as pale as her face. Madame Aubain, at the foot of the cot which she was clutching in her arms, was gasping in agony. The Mother Superior was standing, on the right. Three candlesticks on the chest of drawers made red streaks, and fog whitened the windows. Nuns led away Madame Aubain.

For two nights, Félicité did not leave the dead girl. She repeated the same prayers, poured holy water on the sheets, came back to sit down, and studied her. At the end of her first vigil, she noticed that the face had become yellow, the lips were turning blue, the nose was becoming pinched, the eyes were sinking in. She kissed them many times, and would not have felt any immense surprise if Virginie had reopened them; for such souls the supernatural is simple. She washed her, wrapped her with her shroud, lowered her into her coffin, put a wreath on her head, spread out her hair. It was blond, and extraordinarily long for her age. Félicité cut off a thick lock, half of which she slipped into her bosom, resolved never to be parted from it.

The body was brought back to Pont-l'Évêque, following the wishes of Madame Aubain, who followed the hearse in a closed carriage.

After the Mass, it took another three-quarters of an hour to reach the cemetery. Paul walked at the head and sobbed. M. Bourais was behind, then the chief townspeople, then the women, covered with black mantles, and then Félicité. She was thinking of her nephew, and having been unable to render him these honors, felt an additional sadness, as if they were burying him along with the other.

Madame Aubain's despair was boundless.

First she rebelled against God, thinking him unjust for taking away her daughter—she who had never sinned, and whose conscience was so pure! But no! She should have taken her away to the Midi. Other doctors would have saved her! She blamed herself, wanted to join her, cried out in distress in the midst of her dreams. One dream, especially, haunted her. Her husband, dressed as a sailor, was returning from a long voyage, and, crying, was telling her he had received the order to take Virginie away. So they set about trying to find a hiding-place somewhere.

Once, she came in from the garden, shattered. A moment before, the father and daughter had appeared to her (she pointed to the place) one next to the other; they did nothing; they just looked at her.

For several months, she remained in her room, inert. Félicité lectured her gently; she should keep herself up for her son, and for the other one, in memory "of her."

"Her?" Madame Aubain repeated, as if she were waking up. "Ah! Yes!... Yes!... You never forget her!" This was an allusion to the cemetery, from which she herself had been scrupulously forbidden.

Every day Félicité would go there.

At four o'clock precisely, she would go past the houses, climb the hill, open the gate, and arrive at Virginie's tomb. This was a little column of pink marble, with a slab at the base, and chains around it enclosing a little garden. The raised beds disappeared beneath a blanket of flowers. She watered their leaves, refreshed the sand, knelt down the better to work the earth. When Madame Aubain was finally able to go there, she felt a relief, a kind of consolation.

Then the years flowed by, all the same and without any episodes other than the return of the major feast-days: Easter, Assumption, All Saints. Domestic events stood out, on which they would reflect later on. For instance, in 1825, two glaziers whitewashed the hallway; in 1827, a section of the roof, falling into the courtyard, almost killed a man. The summer of 1828 was the time when Madame presented the offering of the consecrated bread; Bourais around this time was mysteriously absent; and little by little old acquaintances passed away: Guyot, Liébard, Madame Lechaptois, Robelin, Uncle Gremanville, who had long been paralyzed.

One night in Pont-l'Évêque, the driver of the mail-coach announced the July Revolution. A new sub-prefect was named a few days later: the Baron de Larsonnière, formerly a consul in America, who had at home, besides his wife, his sister-in-law with three girls, already quite big. They could be seen on their lawn, dressed in flowing blouses; they owned a black man and a parrot. Madame Aubain received their visit, and did not fail to return it. As soon as they appeared in the far distance, Félicité would run to warn her. But only one thing was capable of moving her: the letters from her son.

He couldn't pursue any career, too absorbed in taverns. She paid his debts for him; he incurred others; and the sighs that Madame Aubain emitted, knitting by the window, reached Félicité, who was turning her spinning wheel in the kitchen.

They strolled together alongside the espalier, and always chatted about Virginie, wondering if such or such a thing would have pleased her, what she might have said on such or such an occasion.

All her little things took up a cupboard in the room with two beds. Madame Aubain examined them as little as possible. One summer day, she resigned herself to the task; and moths flew out of the wardrobe.

Her dresses were lined up under a shelf where there were three dolls, some hoops, a dollhouse, and a washbasin she used to use. They also took out petticoats, stockings, handkerchiefs, and spread them out on the two cots, before folding them. The sun lit up these poor objects, letting stains be seen, and the creases formed by the body's movements. The air outside was hot and blue, a blackbird was chirping, everything seemed to be living in a profound gentleness. They found a little plush hat, with long hairs on it, chestnut colored; but it was all eaten by insects. Félicité asked for it for herself. Their eyes locked on each other, filled with tears; finally the mistress opened her arms, the servant threw herself into them; and they clasped each other, quenching their grief in a kiss that made them equals.

That was the first time in their life, since Madame Aubain was not of an expansive nature. Félicité was grateful to her for it as for a kind deed, and henceforth cherished her with an animal devotion and a religious veneration.

The goodness of her heart grew.

When she heard the drums of a regiment marching in the street, she would stand in front of the door with a jug of cider, and offer drinks to the soldiers. She took care of cholera patients. She gave shelter to the Polish refugees, and there was even one of them who said he wanted to marry her. But they quarreled; for one morning, returning after the angelus, she found him in her kitchen, where he had let himself in, and had prepared himself a cold dish he was calmly eating.

After the Poles, it was old man Colmiche, a dotard who was thought to have committed horrors in '93. He lived on the river's edge, in the ruins of a pigsty. The little boys looked at him through the cracks in the wall, and threw pebbles at him that fell onto his pallet, where he was lying, constantly shaken with catarrh, with very long hair, inflamed eyelids, and on his arm a tumor bigger than his head. She brought him linen, tried to clean his hovel, dreamed of setting him up in the bake-house, if it wouldn't annoy Madame. When the cancer had burst, she bandaged him every day, sometimes brought him biscuits, put him in the sun on a bale of straw; and the poor old man, drooling and trembling, thanked her with his feeble voice, afraid of losing her, stretched out his hands as soon as he saw her moving away. He died; she had a Mass said for the repose of his soul.

On that very day, a great happiness came to her: at dinner-time, Madame de Larsonnière's black man appeared, holding the parrot in its cage, with its perch, chain, and padlock. A note from the Baroness announced to Madame Aubain that, since her husband was promoted to a prefecture, they were leaving that evening; and she begged her to accept this bird, as a souvenir, and as a token of her regard.

For a long time it had occupied Félicité's imagination, for it came from America, and this word reminded her of Victor, so much that she would keep asking the black man about it. Once she had even said, "Madame would be so happy to have it!"

The black man had repeated the statement to his mistress, who, being unable to take it with her, got rid of it in this way.

IV

His name was Loulou. His body was green, the tip of his wings pink, his face blue, and his breast golden.

But he had a tiresome habit of chewing his perch, would tear out his feathers, scatter his droppings, spill his bathwater; Madame Aubain, whom he annoyed, gave him to Félicité for good.

She set about training him; soon he repeated, "Pretty boy! Your servant, Monsieur! Hail Mary full of grace!" He was put near the door, and many people were surprised he didn't answer to the name of Jacquot, since all parrots were named Jacquot. People compared him to a turkey, to a block of wood: so many stabs in the heart for

Félicité! Strange obstinacy Loulou had, to stop speaking the minute people started looking at him!

Nonetheless he sought company; for on Sundays, while the Rochefeuille ladies, M. de Houppeville, and the new regulars—Onfroy the apothecary, M. Varin, and Captain Mathieu—had their card parties, he would beat against the panes with his wings, and thrash about so furiously that it was impossible to hear each other.

Bourais's face must have seemed very amusing to him. As soon as he saw him, he began to laugh, to laugh with all his might. His screams rebounded in the courtyard, the echo repeated them, the neighbors went to their windows and laughed too; in order not to be seen by the parrot, M. Bourais would slip along the wall, hiding his profile with his hat, reach the river, then enter through the garden door. And the looks he gave the bird were lacking in tenderness.

Loulou had been slapped at by the butcher boy, when the bird dared to thrust his head into his basket; and since then he always tried to nip him through his shirt. Fabu threatened to wring his neck, even though he was not cruel, despite the tattoos on his arms and his big side whiskers. Quite the contrary! He had a liking for the parrot, and even wanted, when he was in a jovial mood, to teach him swear words. Félicité, who was frightened by these manners, put him in the kitchen. His chain was taken away, and he wandered throughout the house.

When he went down the stairs, he would lean the curve of his beak against the steps, lift his right foot, then his left; and she was afraid that such gymnastics would cause him dizzy spells. He became ill, could no longer speak or eat. There was a thickness under his tongue, like the kind chickens sometimes have. She cured him by pulling out this film with her fingernails. M. Paul, one day, had the imprudence to blow cigar smoke into his nostrils; another time when Madame Lormeau teased him with the tip of her parasol, he grabbed at the ferrule; to cap it all off, he got lost.

She had put him down on the grass to refresh him, and had gone away for a minute; and, when she returned, no more parrot! First she looked for him in the bushes, by the water's edge and on the roofs, without listening to her mistress who shouted, "Be careful! You're mad!" Then she investigated all the gardens of Pont-l'Évêque; and she stopped passersby: "You haven't, by any chance, happened to see my parrot?" For those who did not know her parrot, she provided a description. All of a sudden, she thought she could make out, behind the windmills, at the base of the hill, a green thing that was fluttering about. But on top of the hill, nothing! A peddler asserted he had seen it not long ago, in Saint-Melaine, in old Mother Simon's shop. She ran there. They didn't know what she was talking about. Finally she returned home, exhausted, her shoes in tatters, death in her soul; and, sitting in the middle of the bench, next to Madame, she was telling her about all her attempts, when a light weight fell on her shoulder: Loulou! What the devil had he been doing? Perhaps he had been strolling about in the neighborhood!

She had difficulty getting over it, or rather she never got over it.

As a consequence of a chill, she got a throat infection; soon afterwards, an earache. Three years later, she was deaf; and she spoke very loudly, even in church. Although her sins could be spread to every corner of the diocese without dishonor for her or awkwardness for everyone else, the priest thought it suitable to hear her confession only in the sacristy.

Illusory buzzing sounds ended up confusing her. Often her mistress said to her, "My God! How stupid you are!" and she replied, "Yes, Madame," looking for something nearby.

The little circle of her ideas grew even smaller, and the peal of the bells, the lowing of the oxen, did not exist any more. All beings functioned with the silence of phantoms. One single noise reached her ears now, the voice of the parrot.

As if to amuse her, he would mimic the click-clack of the roasting spit, the shrill cry of a fish vendor, the saw of the carpenter who lived across the way; and, at the sound of the doorbell, imitated Madame Aubain: "Félicité! The door! The door!"

They had conversations, he, uttering over and over the three phrases in his repertoire, and she, replying with words that were no more connected than they, but in which her heart poured forth. Loulou, in her isolation, was almost a son, a lover. He climbed up her fingers, nibbled at her lips, held on to her kerchief; and, when she tilted her head forward and shook it the way nannies do, the large wings of the bonnet and the wings of the bird quivered together.

When clouds piled up and thunder rumbled, he cried out, remembering perhaps the rainshowers of his native forests. The streaming sound of water roused him to a frenzy; he fluttered about distraught, flew up to the ceiling, overturned everything, and went out the window to splash about in the garden; but returned quickly onto one of the andirons, and, hopping to dry his feathers, showed now his tail, now his beak.

One morning during the terrible winter of 1837, when she had put him in front of the fireplace, because of the cold, she found him dead, in the middle of his cage, with his head down, his talons in the wires. A congestion had killed him, surely? She thought he had been poisoned by parsley; and, despite the absence of any proof, her suspicions rested on Fabu.

She cried so much that her mistress said to her, "Well, have him stuffed!"

She asked advice of the pharmacist, who had always been kind to the parrot.

He wrote to Le Havre. A certain Fellacher undertook such work. But, since the coach sometimes lost parcels, she resolved to carry him herself as far as Honfleur.

Leafless apple trees lined the side of the road. Ice covered the ditches. Dogs barked near the farms and with her hands under her short cape, with her little black clogs and her straw market basket, she walked briskly, in the middle of the road.

She crossed the forest, passed Haut-Chêne, reached Saint-Gatien.

Behind her, in a cloud of dust and carried away by the descent, a mail coach at full gallop was hurtling forward like a whirlwind. Seeing this woman who wasn't moving aside, the driver stood up on the box, and the postilion shouted also, while his four horses which he couldn't hold back accelerated their pace; the two horses in front brushed against her; with a jerk of his reins, he pulled them to the side, but, furious, raised his arm, and in full flight, with his big whip, lashed her from her stomach to her bonnet with such a blow that she fell on her back.

Her first gesture, when she regained consciousness, was to open her basket. Loulou was unhurt, fortunately. She felt a burning on her right cheek; the hands she brought to it were red. The blood flowed.

She sat down on a heap of gravel, dabbed her face with her handkerchief, then ate a crust of bread, which she had put in her basket just in case, and consoled herself for her wound by looking at the bird.

When she arrived at the top of Ecquemauville, she saw the lights of Honfleur sparkling in the night like so many stars; the sea, further on, stretched vaguely out. Then a moment of weakness stopped her; and the misery of her childhood, the disappointment of her first love, the departure of her nephew, the death of Virginie, like the waves of a flood, returned all at once, and, rising up to her throat, stifled her.

Later she asked to speak to the captain of the boat; and, without saying what she was sending, gave him the instructions.

Fellacher kept the parrot a long time. He kept promising it for the following week; after six months, he announced that a crate had been shipped; and there was no more talk of it. It made one think Loulou would never return. "They have stolen him from me!" she thought.

Finally he arrived—and he was gorgeous, erect on a tree branch, which was screwed down on a mahogany pedestal, one foot in the air, his head tilted to the side, chewing on a nut, which the taxidermist, out of a love for the grandiose, had gilded.

She locked him up in her bedroom.

This place, to which she admitted few people, resembled both a chapel and a bazaar, so many religious objects and miscellaneous things did it contain.

A big wardrobe made it difficult to open the door. Opposite the window overlooking the garden, a bull's-eye window looked out on the courtyard; a table, next to the trestle bed, held a water jug, two combs, and a cube of blue soap in a chipped dish. One saw on the walls: rosaries, medals, several pretty Virgins, a holy water stoup made of coconut shell; on the chest of drawers, covered with a sheet like an altar, the shell box Victor had given her; then a watering can and a ball, penmanship notebooks, the illustrated geography book, a pair of girl's boots; and on the mirror stud, hooked on by its ribbons, the little plush hat! Félicité carried this sort of respect so far that she kept one of Monsieur's frock coats. All the old things that

Madame Aubain didn't want, she took for her room. That is why there were artificial flowers on the edge of the dresser, and the portrait of the Comte d'Artois in the recess of the dormer window.

By means of a small shelf, Loulou was placed over a part of the fireplace that came forward into the room. Every morning, when she woke up, she saw him in the dawn light, and remembered then the days gone by, and insignificant actions down to their least details, without grief, full of tranquility.

Communicating with no one, she lived in a sleepwalker's torpor. The processions on Corpus Christi would revive her. She would go to the neighbors' houses to look for candles and straw matting, to decorate the altar of repose they were setting up in the street.

At church, she would always gaze at the Holy Ghost, and noted that it had something of the parrot about it. Its resemblance seemed even more obvious to her on the brightly colored Épinal lithograph that represented the baptism of Our Lord. With its purple wings and emerald body, it really was the spitting image of Loulou.

Having bought it, she hung it up in place of the Comte d'Artois—so that, with one glance, she saw them both together. They became associated in her thoughts, the parrot being sanctified by this relationship to the Holy Ghost, who became more alive and intelligible in her eyes. The Father, to express himself, had not chosen a dove, since those animals have no voice, but rather one of the ancestors of Loulou. And Félicité prayed while looking at the image, but from time to time would turn a little towards the bird.

She wanted to join the Sisters of the Blessed Virgin. Madame Aubain dissuaded her.

An important event arose: Paul's marriage.

After having been first a notary's clerk, then in trade, then in the Customs, then in Taxation, and even having taken steps to enter Streams and Forests, at thirty-six years of age, all of a sudden, by an inspiration from heaven, he had discovered his calling—the Registry Office!—and had shown such marked aptitude for it that an inspector had offered him his daughter, promising him his patronage.

Paul, who had become serious, brought her to his mother's house.

She slighted the customs of Pont-l'Évêque, acted the princess, wounded Félicité. At her departure, Madame Aubain felt relieved.

The following week, they learned of the death of M. Bourais, in Lower Brittany, at an inn. The rumor of suicide was confirmed; doubts were raised as to his integrity. Madame Aubain studied her accounts, and soon discovered the litany of his iniquities: diversions of arrears, concealed sales of timber, false bills, etc. What was more, he had a natural child, and "relations with a person from Dozulé."

These base acts afflicted her greatly. In March 1853, she was taken with a pain in her chest; her tongue looked like it was covered with smoke; leeches didn't relieve the oppression; and on the ninth evening she expired, at the age of only seventy-two.

People had thought her not so old, because of her brown hair, the loops of which surrounded her pale face, marked by smallpox. Few friends missed her, since her manners were of a loftiness that distanced her from others.

Félicité mourned her, as masters have seldom been mourned. That Madame had died before her disturbed her ideas; it seemed to her contrary to the order of things, inadmissible and monstrous.

Ten days later (the time needed to hasten from Besançon), the heirs arrived. The daughter-in-law went through her drawers, chose some furniture, sold others; then they returned to their Registry Office.

Madame's armchair, her pedestal table, her foot-warmer, the eight chairs, were gone! The places where engravings had been were outlined by yellow squares in the middle of the walls. They had taken away the two cots, with their mattresses, and in the closet you could see nothing more of all of Virginie's things! Félicité climbed the stairs, dazed with sadness.

The next day there was a notice on the door: the apothecary shouted into her ear that the house was for sale.

She tottered, and had to sit down.

What mainly filled her with despair was abandoning her bedroom—so convenient for poor Loulou. Enveloping him with a look of anguish, she implored the Holy Ghost, and formed the idolatrous habit of saying her prayers kneeling in front of the parrot. Sometimes, the sun entering through the dormer window struck his glass eye, and made a luminous ray flash forth that threw her into ecstasy.

She had a pension of three hundred and eighty francs, bequeathed by her mistress. The garden provided her with vegetables. As to clothes, she had enough to dress herself till the end of her days, and saved on lighting by going to bed at twilight.

She hardly ever went out, in order to avoid the second-hand shop, where a few of the old pieces of furniture were on display. From the time of her deafness, she had dragged one leg; and her strength diminishing. Old Mother Simon, who had been ruined in the grocery business, came every morning to split her wood and pump the water.

Her eyes became weaker. The shutters were no longer opened. A good many years passed. And the house was not rented, and was not sold.

Out of fear they would send her away, Félicité did not request any repairs. The roof slats were rotting; for an entire winter her bolster was wet. After Easter, she spat blood.

Then Mother Simon had recourse to a doctor. Félicité wanted to know what she had. But, too deaf to hear, one single word reached her: "Pneumonia." It was known to her, and she replied gently, "Ah! Like Madame," finding it natural to follow her mistress.

The time for the altars of repose was approaching.

The first was always at the bottom of the hill, the second in front of the post office, the third towards the middle of the street. There were rivalries about that; and the parishioners finally chose Madame Aubain's courtyard.

The oppressions and the fever increased. Félicité was distressed at being unable to do anything for the altar. If only she could have put something on it! Then she thought of the parrot. This was not suitable, objected the neighbors. But the priest granted his permission; she was so happy that she begged him to accept, when she was dead, Loulou, her only wealth.

From Tuesday to Saturday, the vigil of the Feast of the Blessed Sacrament, she coughed more frequently. In the evening her face was contracted, her lips stuck to her gums, she began to vomit;

and the next day, at daybreak, feeling very low, she had a priest called.

Three old women surrounded her during Extreme Unction. Then she announced she needed to speak to Fabu.

He arrived in his Sunday clothes, ill at ease in this gloomy atmosphere.

"Forgive me," she said with an effort to stretch out her arms; "I thought it was you who had killed him!"

What did she mean by such prattle? Suspecting him of a murder, a man like him! And he became indignant, and would have made a row.

"She's no longer in her right mind, you can see that clearly!"

From time to time Félicité spoke to the shadows. The old women retired. Mother Simon had lunch.

A little later, she picked up Loulou, and, bringing him close to Félicité, said, "Come, now! Say goodbye to him!"

Even though it was not a corpse, worms were eating it; one of its wings was broken, oakum was coming out of its stomach. But, blind now, she kissed his face, and held him against her cheek. Mother Simon took it back, to put it on the altar.

V

The pastures were sending forth their summer fragrances; the flies were buzzing, the sun made the river gleam and warmed the roof tiles. Mother Simon, having returned to the bedroom, gently fell asleep.

The ringing of the bells woke her; they were coming from vespers. Félicité's delirium fell away. Thinking about the procession, she could see it, as if she were following it.

All the schoolchildren, all the choir and the firemen walked on the sidewalks, while in the middle of the street proceeded: first the verger armed with his halberd, the beadle with a large cross, the schoolteacher watching over the children, the nun anxious about her little girls; three of the prettiest, curly-haired like angels, were throwing rose petals in the air; the deacon, his arms spread apart, conducted the music; and two thurifers at each step turned toward the Blessed Sacrament, which was being carried, under a canopy of dark red velvet held up by four churchwardens, by the priest, in his beautiful chasuble. A flood of people brought up the rear, between the white cloths that covered the walls of houses; and they arrived at the bottom of the hill.

A cold sweat moistened Félicité's temples. Mother Simon sponged her with a cloth, telling herself that one day we all have to go that way.

The murmur of the crowd swelled, was very loud for a moment, grew distant.

A fusillade shook the windowpanes. It was the postilions saluting the monstrance. Félicité rolled up her eyes, and she said, as loudly as she could:

"Is he all right?", worried about the parrot.

Her death throes began. A rattle, becoming more and more rapid, made her ribs heave. Bubbles of foam appeared at the corners of her mouth, and her whole body trembled.

Soon, they could make out the roar of the bass horns, the clear voices of the children, the deep voice of the men. Everything became silent now and again, and the patter of footsteps, deadened by flowers, sounded like a flock on the grass.

All the clergy appeared in the courtyard. Mother Simon climbed up onto a chair to reach the bull's-eye window, and in this way looked down on the altar of repose.

Green garlands hung on the altar, which was decorated with a frill of English lace. In the middle there was a little box that held relics, two orange trees in the corners, and, all along it, silver candles and porcelain vases, from which sprung sunflowers, lilies, peonies, foxglove, clusters of hydrangeas. This heap of brilliant colors slanted down, from the first tier to the rug spread on the pavement; and rare things attracted the eye. A silver gilt sugar-bowl had a crown of violets, pendants made of precious Alençon stones sparkled on moss, two Chinese screens showed their landscapes. Loulou, hidden beneath some roses, let only his blue face be seen, like a plaque of lapis lazuli.

The churchwardens, the choir, the children lined up on the three sides of the courtyard. The priest slowly climbed the steps, and placed his great shining golden sun on the lace. Everyone knelt. There was a great silence. And the censers, swinging in full flight, slipped along their chains.

An azure vapor rose up into Félicité's bedroom. She widened her nostrils, breathing it in with a mystical sensuality; then closed her eyes. Her lips smiled. The movements of her heart slowed down little by little, more uncertain, more gentle each time, the way a fountain runs dry, the way an echo disappears; and, when she exhaled her last breath, she thought she saw, as the skies parted, a giant parrot, hovering above her head.